WRECK-IT RALPH

Sugar Rush

By
Ellen O'Hara

Illustrated by
Cory Loftis

A Random House PICTUREBACK® Book

Random House 🏠 New York

Copyright © 2012 Disney Enterprises, Inc. All rights reserved. Published in the United States by Random House Children's Books, a division of Random House, Inc., 1745 Broadway, New York, NY 10019, and in Canada by Random House of Canada Limited, Toronto, in conjunction with Disney Enterprises, Inc. Pictureback, Random House, and the Random House colophon are registered trademarks of Random House, Inc.

randomhouse.com/kids
ISBN: 978-0-7364-2959-7
Printed in the United States of America
10 9 8 7 6 5 4 3 2 1

Hreck-It Ralph worked as the Bad Guy in a video game. At the start of each new game, Ralph yelled, "I'M GONNA WRECK IT!" And then he did.

Fix-It Felix worked as the Good Guy. He fixed everything Ralph wrecked.

The Nicelanders loved Felix. They gave him medals and pies—but they threw Ralph in the mud.

One night, Ralph had an idea: if he got a medal, he could be a Good Guy! But he would have to get it from another game.

Ralph found a medal, but on his way home, he crash-landed in a racing game called Sugar Rush.

A girl named Vanellope saw the medal and cried, "Race you for it!"

"Give it back!"

Ralph demanded.

But Vanellope held on to it. She thought the medal was a gold coin. She wanted to use it to enter the Sugar Rush kart race!

When Ralph finally found Vanellope, she was
in a mud puddle. The other racers had wrecked
her kart.

"Hey, leave her alone!" Ralph shouted. No
one deserved the mud puddle treatment.

Ralph chased the kids away. When he
returned, Vanellope offered him a deal. If he
helped her build a new kart, she would return
his medal when she won the race. Reluctantly,
Ralph agreed.

Vanellope and Ralph sneaked into the Kart Bakery. They were allowed to make two mistakes, but if they made a third, a mallet would smash their kart to pieces!

First, Ralph and Vanellope made the batter.
It was harder to mix than they thought.

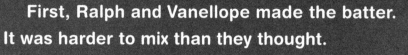

"Too much batter!"

a game voice announced. It was their
first mistake.

Vanellope broke the mixer. That was their second mistake!

"I'm gonna mix it!"

Ralph said, pounding the batter with his huge fists. Then into the oven it went.

At last, a fully baked kart popped out!

"We still have to decorate it," Vanellope said.

They tried to frost the kart but ended up making a gooey mess.

They had made too many mistakes!

"Fail!" the game voice boomed.

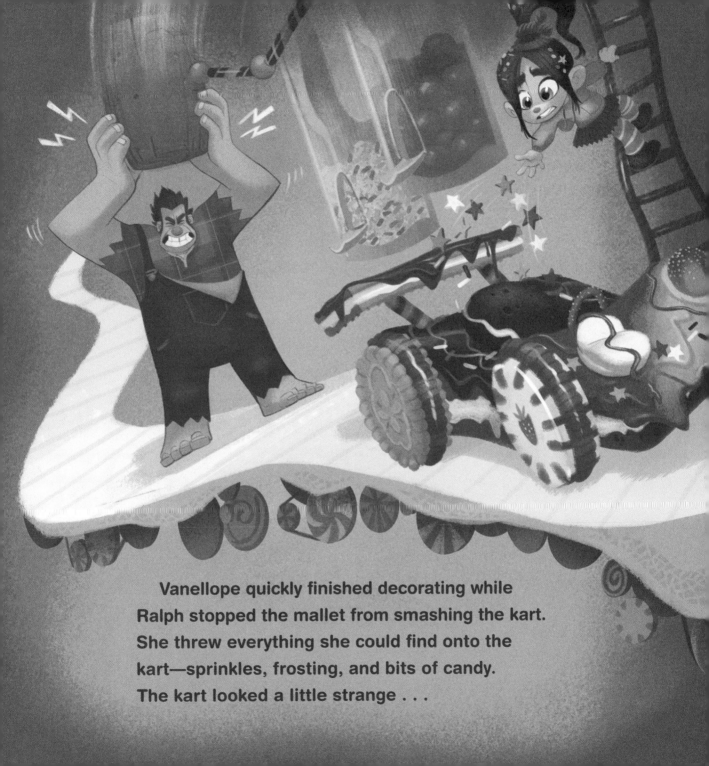

Vanellope quickly finished decorating while
Ralph stopped the mallet from smashing the kart.
She threw everything she could find onto the
kart—sprinkles, frosting, and bits of candy.
The kart looked a little strange . . .

. . . but Vanellope loved it.

"It's perfect!" she cried. She and Ralph proudly signed their names on the side.

There was still one problem. "I don't know how to drive a real kart," Vanellope said.

"If you're gonna race, you need to learn how to drive," Ralph said. He used his giant fists to pound out some stones so Vanellope could have a practice racetrack.

At last the track was ready, but the kart was still a mystery. Ralph couldn't drive, either!

Vanellope finally got going. Then something strange happened. Vanellope and her kart disappeared—and reappeared in another spot. She had glitched! Ralph thought she might have a chance at winning . . . if only she could stop **glitching!**

Vanellope zoomed around the track. Ralph had to admit she was a natural—maybe even a winner.

"You're doing it!"

he said.

Ralph and Vanellope headed to the Sugar Rush
race. Vanellope was going to be a real racer.
But she no longer wanted to win just for herself.
She wanted to win for Ralph, too.

It was race time, but Vanellope and Ralph were late to the starting line. The other racers had already taken off! Vanellope zoomed ahead.

The other racers bumped into Vanellope's kart, trying to break it, but she was **unstoppable!**

After a few glitches, Ralph helped Vanellope get across the finish line to win back his medal. But Ralph realized he didn't need a medal after all. He already felt like a Good Guy.